A NOTE TO PARENTS

Reading is often considered the most important skill children learn in the primary grades. Much can be done at home to lay the foundation for early reading success.

When they read, children use the following to figure out words: story and picture clues, how a word is used in a sentence, and sound/spelling relationships. The **Hello Reader!** *Phonics Fun* series focuses on sound/spelling relationships through phonics activities. Phonics instruction unlocks the door to understanding sounds and the letters or spelling patterns that represent them.

The **Hello Reader!** *Phonics Fun* series is divided into the following three sets of books, based on important phonic elements:

- **Sci-Fi Phonics**: word families
- **Monster Phonics**: consonants, blends, and digraphs
- **Funny Tale Phonics**: short and long vowels

Learn About Vowels

The Funny Tale Phonics stories, including *The Three Wishes*, feature words that have the same vowel sound. These books help children become aware of and use these sounds when decoding, or sounding out, new words. After reading the book, you might wish to begin lists of words that contain each vowel sound. For example, one list could contain all the short *a* words, another list all the short *i* words, and so on.

Enjoy the Activities

- Challenge your child to build words using the letters and word parts provided. Help your child by demonstrating how to sound out new words.
- Match words with pictures to help your child attach meaning to text.
- Become word detectives by identifying story words with the same vowel sound.
- Keep the activities game-like and praise your child's efforts.

Develop Fluency

Encourage your child to read these books again and again and again. Each time, set a different purpose for reading.

- Point to a word in the story. Say it aloud. Ask your child what sound he or she hears in the middle of the word. Then look at the letter or letters that stand for that sound.
- Suggest to your child that he or she read the book to a friend, family member, or even a pet.

Whatever you do, have fun with the books and instill the joy of reading in your child. It is one of the most important things you can do!

—Wiley Blevins, Reading Specialist
Ed.M., Harvard University

To Gwen
— J.B.S.

To my wife, Martha
— R.F.

Text copyright © 1997 by Judith Bauer Stamper.
Illustrations copyright © 1997 by Ron Fritz.
All rights reserved. Published by Scholastic Inc.
HELLO READER!, CARTWHEEL BOOKS and associated logos
are trademarks and/or registered trademarks of Scholastic Inc.

Library of Congress Cataloging-in-Publication Data

Stamper, Judith Bauer.
    The three wishes / by Judith Bauer Stamper; illustrated by Ron Fritz;
    phonics activities by Wiley Blevins.
        p.   cm.—(Hello reader! Phonics fun. Funny tale phonics)
    "Vowels: short a and short i."
    "Cartwheel Books."
    Summary: A fat cat and a big pig cannot get along until a fairy gives them
four wishes. Includes related phonics activities.
    ISBN 0-590-76266-4
    [1. Pigs—Fiction. 2. Cats—Fiction. 3. Stories in rhyme.] I. Fritz, Ronald,
ill. II. Blevins, Wiley. III. Title. IV. Series.
PZ8.3.S78255Tr   1997
[E]—dc21   97-14517
                                                                            CIP
                                                                            AC

10 9 8 7 6   8 9/9 0/0 01 02
                        Printed in the U.S.A.   23
                    First printing, December 1997

THE Three Wishes

by Judith Bauer Stamper
Illustrated by Ron Fritz
Phonics Activities by Wiley Blevins

Hello Reader! Phonics Fun

Funny Tale Phonics • Vowels: short *a* and short *i*

SCHOLASTIC INC.
New York Toronto London Auckland Sydney

Once there was a cat.
This cat was so fat!

His friend was a pig.
This pig was so big!

The cat's name was Andy.
He thought he was dandy.

The pig's name was Izzy.
She was a bit dizzy.

Their house was so small.
It didn't fit them at all!

They fought day and night.
The noise was a fright!

A fairy passed by
and let out a cry.

"I'll give you three wishes,
if you stop throwing dishes!"

The pig and the cat
stopped having their spat.

But both were still mad.
And their wishes were bad!

The cat wished a wig
on top of the pig.

The pig wished a rat
on top of the cat.

The cat wished a fish
on top of Izzy's dish.

The pig wished a sack
on top of Andy's back.

The cat wished something icky
to make the pig sticky.

The pig wished some ants
to make the cat dance.

The fairy stopped by
and let out a cry.

"You need one wish more.
I'll give you each four!"

No more icky thing, fish, or wig,
wished the cat for the pig.

No more ants, sack, or rat,
wished the pig for the cat.

Then the pig and the cat
had a nice, little chat...

friend to friend.
The End.

•PHONICS ACTIVITIES•
Izzy's Wish

Izzy has one wish. She wants to find every picture whose name has the *i* sound as in *big*. Help make Izzy's wish come true.

Picture Match

Match the picture with its name.
Find the picture's name in the story.

cat

pig

ants

fish

wig

Word Search

Find each picture's name in the word search.

c	a	t	p	f
g	f	d	f	i
p	r	a	t	s
i	d	i	s	h
g	p	c	w	p
r	g	w	i	g

Build a Word

Use the letters in the pans to make new words. Add each letter to the word ending. If it makes a word, say it aloud.

at

ack

ad

ag

an

am

Rhyme Time

Name each picture. Match the pictures whose names rhyme.

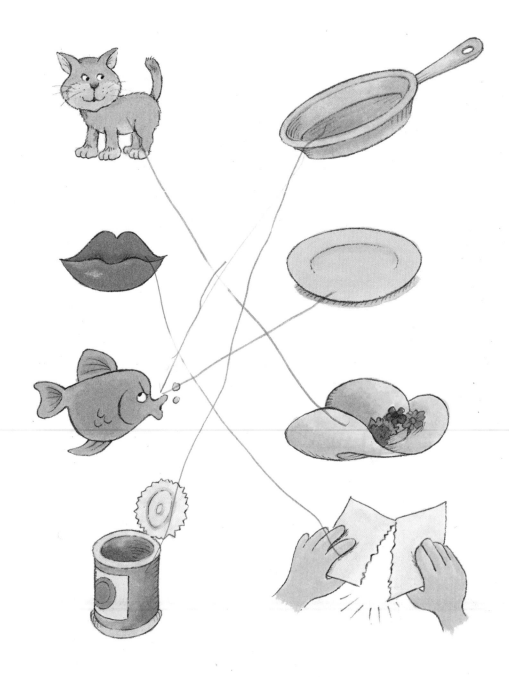

Word Ladders

Use one of the words in the box to finish each word ladder. Each word on the ladder changes by only one letter.

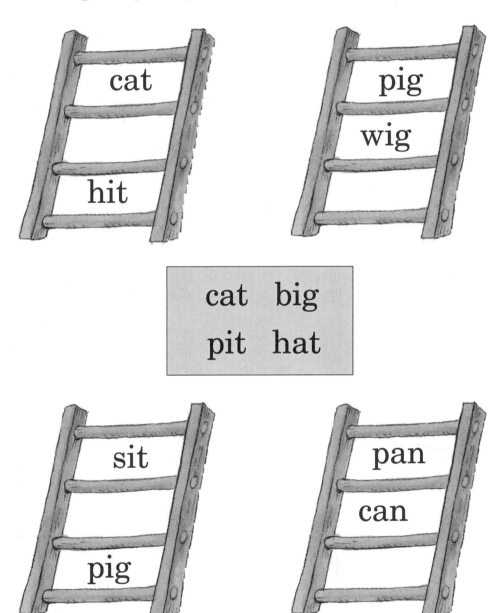

cat

hit

pig

wig

cat   big
pit   hat

sit

pig

pan

can

Answers

Izzy's Wish

Build a Word

bat bad ban back bag bam; pat
pad pan pack; sat sad sack sag;
cat cad can; hat had hack hag
ham; rat rad ran rack rag ram;
tad tan tack tag; man mat mad

Rhyme Time

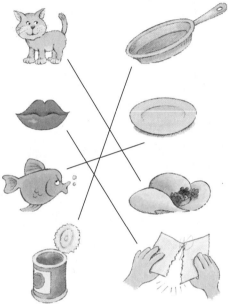

Picture Match

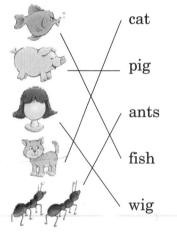

cat

pig

ants

fish

wig

Word Search

c	a	t	p		f
g	f	d	f		i
p	r	a	t		s
i	d	i	s		h
g	p	c	w		p
r	g	w	i	g	

Word Ladders

cat
hat
hit

pig
wig
big

sit
pit
pig

pan
can
cat